I Can Read!™

BEGINNING READING
1

LITTLE BEAR
AND THE MARCO POLO

by Else Holmelund Minarik
pictures by Dorothy Doubleday

HARPER
An Imprint of HarperCollinsPublishers

To Anne and Bill Lester,
my sister and brother-in-law,
with love and gratitude
—E.H.M.

To my daughter Deirdre,
who loved Little Bear
—D.D.

Little Bear and the Marco Polo. Text copyright © 2010 by Else Holmelund Minarik. Illustrations copyright © 2010 by HarperCollins Publishers. All rights reserved. No part of this book may be used or reproduced in any manner whatsoever without written permission except in the case of brief quotations embodied in critical articles and reviews. Manufactured in China. For information address HarperCollins Children's Books, a division of HarperCollins Publishers, 10 East 53rd Street, New York, NY 10022.
www.icanread.com

Library of Congress Cataloging-in-Publication Data is available.
ISBN 978-0-06-085485-0 (trade bdg.) — ISBN 978-0-06-085487-4 (pbk.)

11 12 13 14   SCP   10 9 8 7 6 5   ❖   First Edition

Little Bear was in the garden,

playing with his ladybug,

when Grandmother Bear called,

"Little Bear, Grandfather needs help

in the attic."

Little Bear loved the attic.

He hurried to join Grandfather Bear.

He took Ladybug along.

When Little Bear got to the attic,

Grandfather Bear was sweeping.

What a lot of dust!

They both sneezed. "Achoo, achoo!"

"Let's open the window," said Grandfather.

"I'll do it!" said Little Bear.

He opened the window

and Ladybug flew off.

"Grandfather," said Little Bear,

"my ladybug flew away!"

Grandfather said, "Don't worry.

She'll be back again."

Grandfather Bear said, "Ouch, my back.

I'm growing stiff.

Little Bear, would you help me

open the trunk?"

Little Bear was glad to do it.

They opened the trunk,

and there was a blue jacket

and a fancy blue cap.

Grandfather put the cap

on Little Bear's head.

He draped the jacket

over Little Bear's shoulders.

"There!" he said.

"That makes you a sea captain,

just as I was."

Little Bear found a mirror.

He admired himself.

"Look at me, Grandfather.

Now I am a sea captain,

just like you.

All I need is a ship."

But Grandfather Bear was sitting

in his old chair.

He had dozed off.

Little Bear looked in the trunk again.

He found a picture of a ship.

"Oh," cried Little Bear. "What a fine ship."

That woke Grandfather Bear up.

"Let me see it, Little Bear.

Why, that is my ship.

My own little ship, called the *Marco Polo*."

They both studied the picture.

"Why does it have that name?"

asked Little Bear.

"Because," said Grandfather,
"Marco Polo was a sea captain too,
and he explored the world."

"The world!" Little Bear wondered.

By now Grandfather was wide awake.

He said, "Fetch me the globe over there.

See," said Grandfather,

"the world is round.

The blue is water, and the rest is land."

Little Bear looked at the globe.

"What is all the white?" he asked.

"That," said Grandfather Bear,

"is the North Pole,

where the Polar Bear lives."

Little Bear asked, "If we sailed

there together, what would happen?"

Grandfather laughed.

"I'd shake the Polar Bear's paw,

and you'd shake his paw too."

Little Bear wanted to hear more.

"Where would we sail next?" he asked.

Grandfather Bear said,

"Next we would sail to China

to meet the giant Panda Bear."

"What would he look like?"

asked Little Bear.

"Oh," said Grandfather,

"he is black and white

and very grand indeed!"

"Are there other bears
in other places?" Little Bear asked.
Grandfather Bear said, "In Australia
there are Koala Bears.
We could sail to Australia
and get to meet some.
They live in trees there."
"I could live in trees too!"
said Little Bear.
Grandfather Bear asked,
"But could you also live on leaves?"
Little Bear laughed and shook his head.
"No, thank you."

"But here we are in the attic!"

said Grandfather Bear.

"Let's see what else is in the trunk."

They found a beautiful white dress

and a picture of a lovely young bear

wearing the dress.

Grandfather Bear smiled.

He said, "There she is—

your grandmother wearing this dress."

"She is wonderful," said Little Bear.

"That is what I thought too,"

said Grandfather Bear.

"So I asked her to marry me."

"And she did!" shouted Little Bear.

"Yes, I was very lucky!"

said his grandfather.

Little Bear asked,

"And then, did you go

sailing around the world together?"

"No-o-o," said Grandfather Bear.

"Grandmother Bear wanted

to build a house first.

Our friends the raccoons

helped us build it."

"And afterward, did you go around
the world together?" asked Little Bear.
"No-o-o," said Grandfather Bear.
"Because then we had to plant
the fruit trees and the berry bushes."
Little Bear was silent.

Little Bear leaned

on Grandfather's lap.

He looked up at Grandfather and said,

"I do like fruits and berries,

but I wonder about the *Marco Polo*.

Where is the *Marco Polo* now?"

"The *Marco Polo* is in dry dock,"
said Grandfather Bear.
"Do you want to see it?"
Yes, Little Bear wanted to see
the *Marco Polo* with all his heart.
On the way through the kitchen
they gave Grandmother Bear
the white dress.
Little Bear said,
"If you put on the dress,
I'll dance with you
when we come back for lunch.
We're going to see the *Marco Polo*."

The *Marco Polo* rested

on a wooden frame by the river.

Some raccoons were washing it down.

Little Bear took a deep breath.

"It's even more beautiful

than I thought," he said.

Grandfather Bear wiped away a tear.

Little Bear climbed aboard.

"Ahoy there," he called to the raccoons.

"I will be your captain."

Little Bear saluted

and the raccoons cheered.

"We will sail around the world.

Just you wait and see!"

And then it was time to go home.

Little Bear took Grandfather Bear's paw.

"You're not sad, are you, Grandfather?"

he asked,

looking up at Grandfather Bear.

No, Grandfather Bear was not sad.

"I'm just plain hungry, Little Bear,"

he said.

Grandmother Bear had a picnic basket
ready and waiting.

She was wearing the white dress.

"Just a mite tight," she said, laughing.

Little Bear looked up at Grandmother,
took her paw, and said, "Lovely lady,
will you marry me?"

"Too late!" said Grandfather Bear.

"She's already mine."

"And," said Grandmother Bear,

"both of you are mine!

You may now help each other carry
the picnic basket out to the garden."

"See, Little Bear," said Grandfather.

"There's no place like home.

Just remember that when you

begin to sail around the world."

Little Bear nodded.

He would have answered,

but his mouth was full of cookie,

a peanut butter and chocolate one!